COMPANY'S COMING

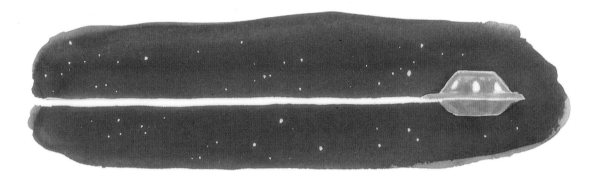

COMPANY'S COMING

by Arthur Yorinks

illustrated by David Small

Dragonfly Books
CROWN PUBLISHERS, INC. • *New York*

A DRAGONFLY BOOK PUBLISHED BY CROWN PUBLISHERS, INC.
Text copyright © 1988 by Arthur Yorinks
Illustrations copyright © 1988 by David Small
Published by Crown Publishers, Inc., a Random House company,
225 Park Avenue South, New York, New York 10003
Originally published in hardcover by Crown Publishers, Inc., in 1988.
CROWN is a trademark of Crown Publishers, Inc.
Manufactured in the United States of America

Library of Congress Cataloging-in-Publication Data
Yorinks, Arthur.
Company's coming.
Summary: Chaos erupts when Moe and Shirley invite some
visitors from outer space to stay for dinner with the relatives.
[1. Extraterrestrial beings–Fiction]   I. Small,
David, 1945–   ill. II. Title.
PZ7.Y819Co. 1988   [E]   87-13579
ISBN 0-517-56751-2 (trade)
0-517-58858-7 (pbk.)

10 9 8 7 6 5 4 3 2 1

First Dragonfly Books edition: October 1992

For Shirley

—A. Y.

For Sherry

—D. S.

On the day Shirley had invited all of her relatives to dinner and Moe, her husband, was pleasantly tinkering in the yard, a flying saucer quietly landed next to their toolshed. Moe was surprised.

"Shirley!" he yelled.

Shirley joined Moe on the patio.

"Moe, you had to buy *that* barbecue? It's too big,"
she complained.

"Shirl, it's not a barbecue," Moe said.

Suddenly, a small hatch on the saucer opened and out walked two visitors from outer space.

"Greetings," they spoke in English. "We come in peace. Do you have a bathroom?"

Stunned, Shirley replied, "Down the hall and to the left." The foreigners nodded graciously and walked into the house.

"How could you let them into our house!" Moe was upset.

"Did you see those helmets? Those ray guns? They'll vaporize us!" Moe was very upset.

"Shhush, they're coming," Shirley whispered.
"Stay calm. Be polite. Maybe we can make friends with
them."

"What a lovely house you have," the strangers commented. "What do you call this place?"

"Bellmore," Shirley politely answered. The visitors nodded.

"We're from away. Far away. And we've been traveling for years on our way to the next galaxy—"

"How about a sandwich, you must be hungry," Shirley nervously interrupted. "Would you like to stay for dinner?"

"Gee!" they replied. "We'd love to. We'll return at six o'clock." The spacemen went back to their ship and flew off. Moe and Shirley ran into the house.

"Are you crazy! The cousins are coming tonight. Why did you invite *them* to dinner?" Moe asked. "They'll atomize us. Bellmore...the whole Earth is doomed, I tell you!" Moe was hysterical.

"Moe, Moe, take it easy. They look like nice boys," Shirley said. "Come, help me make the potato salad."

But Moe had other thoughts. Saying he had to wash his hands, he went upstairs and called the FBI. The FBI called the Pentagon. And the Pentagon called the Army, the Air Force, and the Marines.

At a quarter to six, the house was surrounded.

Inside, the cousins sat, panicked.

"Act natural," Shirley told her relatives. "Be nice. So they look a little different, I'm sure they're friendly," she said, as she served the appetizers.

"Don't worry," Moe added. "If those aliens make one false move, they've had it! So relax."

Moe heard a humming and ran to the window.
"They're here!" he yelled.

The doorbell rang. Everyone froze. Cousin Etta
fainted.

"I'll get it," Shirley called. She went to the door.
"Hello, hello, come right in," she greeted the men
from outer space. They were carrying a box.

"How about a drink, some soda? Are you tired? It's getting late, if you leave now you'll just miss the traffic." Moe tried to usher them out.

"So, guys, what's new, have you been to Venus yet, I hear it's hot in the summer," Cousin Sheldon the loudmouth asked. The spacemen sat.

"Well, we're on our way to check out a new planet. Our population has grown so quickly that we must branch out and find new places to live; know what I mean?"

"Sure, we know what you mean," Moe blurted out. "An invasion—we're doomed," he whispered to Cousin Harriet.

"Dinner!" Shirley called.

"Oh, please, before dinner, we have something for you. It'll knock you out." The visitors presented their box.

"It's a bomb! It's gas! It's a laser!" Etta yelled and then fainted again. Soldiers burst into the house. Tanks pointed their guns.

Shirley gingerly began to unwrap the gift. "We weren't sure if you had one of these," the men started to say.

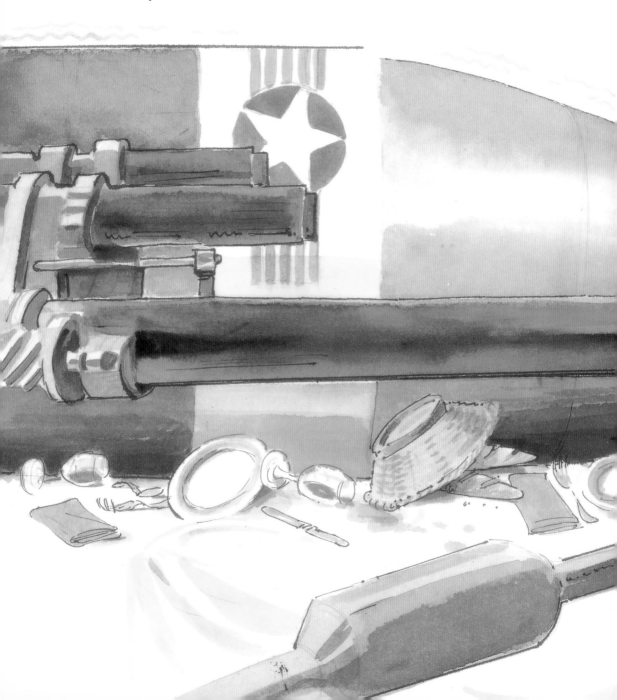

Shirley interrupted. "It's a, it's a, it's a—" The cousins were paralyzed.

"It's a, it's a," Shirley continued. Moe was sweating from head to foot. "OH!" Shirley blurted. Etta, Moe, and Sheldon fainted.

"It's a *blender*!" Shirley declared.
"And we don't even have one."

"We thought you'd like it. And it was on sale!"
The spacemen beamed. Shirley went over and kissed
them both. "Let's eat!" she said.

Luckily, Shirley had made extra spaghetti and meatballs. The cousins, the soldiers, the pilots, the Marines, the FBI men—everyone sat down and had a delicious meal; from soup to nuts.